K:
Choose Y...

"I like *Choose Your Own Adventure* because it feels like you're actually in the real book."

Alexander Rivera, age 9

"These books are great because if you make one choice, you go one way, if you go another way, something else happens!"

Cooper Rappeport, age 10

"I love this book series because it is like you are making and experiencing the book. When you have made a mistake, you can just go back and choose a new adventure or you can just hope for the best."

Nell Pearson, age 8

"*Choose Your Own Adventure* is like you are literally in the book. And it's like you are writing your own book. When I make a bad decision, I can turn back to make a better decisi... make friends throughou... The End.

Lucy Badger,

CHECK OUT CHOOSE YOUR OWN NIGHTMARE:
EIGHTH GRADE WITCH
BLOOD ISLAND • SNAKE INVASION

YOU MIGHT ALSO ENJOY THESE BESTSELLERS...

CHOOSE YOUR OWN ADVENTURE®

THE THRONE
OF ZEUS

BY DEBORAH LERME GOODMAN

ILLUSTRATED BY MARCO CANNELLA

CHOOSECO

WAITSFIELD, VERMONT

Illustrated by: Marco Cannella
Cover illustrated by: Marco Cannella
Book design: Stacey Boyd, Big Eyedea Visual Design

For information regarding permission, write to:

CHOOSECO
P.O. Box 46
Waitsfield, Vermont 05673
www.cyoa.com

Publisher's Cataloging-In-Publication Data
Names: Goodman, Deborah Lerme, 1956- | Cannella, Marco, illustrator. |
Cannella, Marco, illustrator.
Title: The throne of Zeus / by Deborah Lerme Goodman ; illustrated by
Marco Cannella ; cover illustrated by Marco Cannella.
Other Titles: Choose your own adventure.
Description: [Revised edition]. | Waitsfield, Vermont : Chooseco,
[2018] | Originally published: New York : Bantam Books, ©1984. Choose
your own adventure ; 40. | Summary: You've been magically transported
back to ancient Greece by the goddess Athena. Your task is to find
Zeus, king of Olympus.
Identifiers: ISBN 1937133303 | ISBN 9781937133306
Subjects: LCSH: Zeus (Greek deity)—Juvenile fiction. | Missing persons—
Juvenile fiction. | Greece—Juvenile fiction. | CYAC: Zeus (Greek
deity)—Juvenile fiction. | Missing persons—Fiction. | Greece—Fiction. |
LCGFT: Fantasy fiction. | Action and adventure fiction. | Choose-your-
own stories.
Classification: LCC PZ7.G61358 Th 2018 | DDC [Fic]—dc23

Published simultaneously in the United States and Canada

Printed in Canada

10 9 8 7 6 5 4 3 2 1

To Gram, for your stories and devotion

BEWARE and WARNING!

This book is different from other books.

You and YOU ALONE are in charge of what happens in this story.

There are dangers, choices, adventures, and consequences. YOU must use all of your numerous talents and much of your enormous intelligence. The wrong decision could end in disaster—even death. But don't despair. At any time, YOU can go back and make another choice, alter the path of your story, and change its result.

Your parents have unearthed the fabled throne of Zeus in an archaeological dig near Athens, Greece, but they cannot prove it! You travel back in time to ask Zeus himself for the evidence. But reaching Zeus is not as easy as it sounds...along the way, you may battle the ferocious Minotaur, soar through the skies with Icarus, join Hercules on his perilous escapades, attempt to rescue Persephone from the merciless Hades, or drive the Chariot of the Sun, if you dare...good luck!

For months, you and your grandmother have waited for your parents to return home to Athens. Their archaeological digs often take them to distant parts of Greece, but they have never been gone so long before. Your mother and father have unearthed a throne they believe was made for the ancient Greek god Zeus. They're convinced it is the first trace ever discovered of Olympus, palace of the gods. You were eager to hear about their excavations and see pictures of the throne, but now that your parents are home, they seem upset.

"The university has threatened to discontinue the excavation," says your father. "We need hard evidence by the end of the summer to convince them that this throne could only have been made for Zeus."

"What kind of evidence?" you ask.

Turn to the next page.

2

"We need something that clearly links the throne to Zeus. A crown inscribed with his name would help. A stone tablet listing the laws of Olympus would be ideal, but we don't know if such a thing ever existed," your mother answers.

"Talk to Zeus," murmurs your grandmother, clearing the table.

Turn to page 5.

For three days you cling to the plank. The sun scorches your face and arms. You are so parched that you try drinking seawater, but it only makes you feverish and sick. As you slip into unconsciousness, you dream of Zeus.

He sits on a throne that looks just like the one your parents discovered. "I know you want to ask a favor for your parents," Zeus tells you. "However, I will grant them a different wish than the one you had in mind. I will save your life and return you to your own century, but they will have to continue their excavation without my assistance."

Zeus removes a gold ring from his hand and puts it on one of your fingers. The ring is much too big for you, and you have to clench your fingers to keep it from sliding off.

You awaken to the white glare of a hospital room. Your grandmother is sitting beside you. Without a trace of surprise, she points to a massive gold ring on your finger and says, "I see you found Zeus."

The End

"Have *you* ever talked with Zeus?" you ask your grandmother later as you help her wash the dishes.

"A few times," she replies. "On the summer solstice, the ancient gods take special interest in mortal beings. Sometimes they appear on earth. Why, I have even walked with Zeus!"

"Tomorrow is the solstice," you say, shivering with excitement. "Maybe if I can talk to the gods, I can help Mom and Dad find the evidence they need. Since *they* won't ask Zeus for clues, I'll do it myself! But tell me, Gram, where can I find Zeus?"

"I can't tell you that." She kisses you goodnight. "You have to discover Zeus on your own."

All night, you wonder where you might find Zeus. You can't envision him appearing in your modern apartment, but you can imagine him striding comfortably through an ancient temple. You decide to spend the summer solstice at the Acropolis, the site of the famous temple ruins overlooking Athens.

Turn to the next page.

6

After telling your grandmother of your plans, you wait until late afternoon to go to the Acropolis. There are many tourists snapping pictures of the marble ruins, but you know from previous visits that the guards will usher everyone out at five o'clock. You survey the area as you plan your course of action.

Chain link fences encircle each of the ancient sanctuaries. The Parthenon is the largest, most important temple, and the one you think Zeus would be most likely to visit. Unfortunately, it also attracts the greatest number of people, and you'll have a hard time entering it unseen. Maybe you should try the Sanctuary of Artemis Brauronia. There aren't as many people around it.

If you think it is safer to hide in the Sanctuary of Artemis Brauronia, turn to page 11.

If you decide to sneak into the Parthenon, turn to page 40.

"Close your eyes and I'll take you to Crete. You'll like Icarus," says Athena. Placing her hands on your shoulders, she spins you around until you become almost unbearably dizzy. Finally Athena releases you.

You find yourself in a narrow passage with high stone walls. There is no ceiling, and the sky above you is dazzlingly blue. A startled man and boy, both draped in loose white clothing, are staring at you.

"I've been in the sun too long, Icarus," says the man, rubbing his forehead wearily. "I'm having visions!"

"No, you're not!" you cry. "Athena brought me here to find Zeus."

"You've come to the wrong place if you're looking for Zeus," says the man, bitterly. "I don't suppose Athena sent any water with you, did she?"

You shake your head.

"If this isn't just like the gods," comments the man. "They don't bring you water when you're dying of thirst. No, instead, they bring you a visitor in funny clothes."

"Maybe Athena brought the visitor to help us escape," suggests Icarus. Then he tells you, "Don't mind my father. He's upset about our problem."

"What's wrong?"

Turn to page 15.

"Fine," answers Athena. "I'll take you to Persephone, in the fields of Enna." She grasps your shoulders and twirls you around. Your feet fly off the ground as you spin through a silvery fog. When your body pops into place again, you find yourself in a vast meadow.

A girl about your age looks up from a bed of lilies and says, "That's strange clothing you're wearing. Are you one of Athena's friends from another place in time?"

"Why, yes," you answer, surprised. "Athena brought me here to look for Zeus. Do you ever see him?"

"Quite often," the girl answers. "You've come to the right place. My name is Persephone."

As you and Persephone stroll through the meadow, you see wisps of smoke wafting out of a deep gorge slashed into the earth.

Persephone notices a flower at the edge of the chasm. "I can smell that flower from here!" she cries, and races toward the strange blossom.

Turn to the next page.

10

You sniff the air, but all you smell is the rotten egg stench of sulfur. Suddenly a gleaming black chariot drawn by ebony horses dashes out of the chasm. Without stopping, the driver yanks Persephone into the chariot. You make a dash and hurl yourself in just before the chariot plunges back into the depths of the chasm.

Noticing you, the driver wryly comments, "Very few ever choose to join me."

"Who is he?" you ask Persephone.

"Hades," she whispers. "Lord of the Underworld." Her face has turned deathly white.

Turn to page 16.

Casually you stroll around the remains of the Shrine of Artemis Brauronia, hoping the other visitors will leave soon. At last, when no one is watching, you dart under a half-fallen pillar and wedge yourself between two gigantic blocks of stone. By twisting your neck just a bit, you discover that you have a clear view of the Parthenon across the way.

Although you are extremely uncomfortable, you wait quietly as the guards make their rounds. The setting sun casts a rosy glow on the marble ruins, but you're not in a mood to admire the scenery.

Soon after the moon rises, you notice a soft light radiating from the interior of the Parthenon. At first you think it must come from the flashlight of a night watchman, but then you begin to wonder if it could be Zeus!

If you decide to investigate the source of light, turn to page 13.

If you decide to stay right where you are, turn to page 29.

12

You walk out of Hades's palace toward the gate where Cerberus stands guard. One of his heads is napping, but the other two watch you intently and growl. This wakes the third head. Immediately it bares its teeth too.

Even if Cerberus is quite different from any other dog you've known, you remind yourself that he's still just a dog—though a dog with three heads. You whistle to the beast and slap your hands on your thighs. "Come here, pup!" you call, trying to keep your voice from quavering.

Cerberus saunters over and sniffs your shoulders. Your hands tremble as you reach up, past your head, to pet the beast. He seems to like you!

You break off a branch from a nearby tree and throw it. "Bring me the stick!" you instruct Cerberus. As he romps off to retrieve it, you get an idea!

Turn to page 44.

You run toward the Parthenon and clamber over the fence. Breathlessly you stumble up the steps. Behind the pillars, the light is pale and misty. A tall woman in white robes stands at the center of the temple.

Turn to page 18.

"A few years ago, my father, Daedalus, built this Labyrinth for King Minos to imprison the Minotaur, a horrible beast that is half-bull and half-man," Icarus explains. "Only now King Minos is angry with us, and *we're* stuck in the maze, too."

"There are miles of corridors, but only one way out," adds Daedalus ruefully. "Unless we escape soon, we will die of thirst—or be eaten by the Minotaur."

"Let's get going!" you exclaim. "We've got to get out of here fast!"

"There's no sense in moving about," snaps Daedalus. "At best, you'll only make yourself thirstier, and at worst, you'll meet the Minotaur. Calm down and help us think of a solution."

If you answer, "I'm sorry to leave you, but I want to get on with my search for Zeus," turn to page 20.

If you decide to stay with Icarus and Daedalus, turn to page 24.

16

What have I gotten myself into? you wonder.

The chariot races through grim, gray caverns. Farther ahead, a bizarrely iridescent river shimmers with the only colors in the Underworld landscape.

"The river Styx," murmurs Persephone. "The river of hate." As the horses fly over it, you gaze into the dark water. You're not sure if you bargained for this.

Should you jump into the river Styx and get away, or continue farther into the Underworld with Persephone?

If you remain in the chariot, turn to page 33.

If you leap into the water, turn to page 78.

18

"Welcome to my temple," the woman says warmly as she offers you her hand.

You're too frightened to take it. You barely manage to stammer, "You're not Zeus!"

She laughs. "Of course not! I'm Athena, daughter of Zeus. If you wanted to meet my father, you shouldn't have come to my temple." Gingerly, you take her hand. You are surprised to find that it feels remarkably like your mother's.

"Can you take me to Zeus?" you ask.

"I can bring you back to ancient times, and give you the power to speak and understand the language," Athena offers, "but you'll have to find Zeus on your own."

"How will I know where he is?"

"I can't tell you where to find Zeus," Athena explains. "The trick is to attract his attention by doing something he'll find exciting."

She thinks for a moment. "I know two people who are about to have intriguing experiences. Persephone doesn't know it yet, but she's going to be spending a lot of time with Hades, one of Zeus's brothers. Icarus is on the island of Crete right now, and he's—well, let's just say he has an adventure ahead of him. Would you like me to take you to Persephone or Icarus?"

If you answer, "I'd like to meet Icarus,"
turn to page 7.

If you say, "Please take me to Persephone,"
turn to page 8.

"I'm sorry," you say, "but I can't tell you where the Bull of Minos is."

Hercules scowls with rage. Without a word, he grabs your wrist and begins swinging your body in circles. Excruciating pain shoots up your arm. You wonder if a change of plan might be a good idea—but by then, you're too dizzy to speak.

Suddenly Hercules releases you. With breathtaking speed, you sail through the air. Your body burns fiercely and seems to shatter into several pieces. You lose consciousness.

A new group of stars appears in the sky that night, right beside the constellation of Taurus the Bull. People name the new constellation "Guardian of the Bull," and tell stories about your valiant attempt to resist Hercules.

The End

"Good luck with your search for Zeus," says Daedalus with a trace of scorn. "I have a feeling it's the Minotaur—not a god—that you'll find."

You wander through the Labyrinth without any sense of direction. As the hours pass, you grow thirsty and tired. Just when you begin to wonder if you should have stayed with Icarus and Daedalus, you take another left turn and find yourself facing the strangest creature you've ever seen—the Minotaur!

You freeze with terror. The Minotaur towers above you, equally still. It has the head of a huge black bull, and its body is part bull and part human. You wonder whether you should try to reason with the beast or just run for your life.

If you summon all your courage and offer the Minotaur your hand, turn to page 28.

If you turn on your heels and flee, turn to page 30.

In less than an hour, Hermes returns with Persephone in Hades's chariot. You're relieved to see that she is out of her trance.

"Climb in," Hermes calls to you. The three of you ride past the jagged rocks of the Underworld, over the river Styx, and into the light of day.

After you return Persephone to the field where you found her, Hermes turns to you. "Where shall I take you, my friend?"

"I would like to meet Zeus." You describe your parents' discovery of the throne of Zeus.

Hermes stares at you intently. "You say you live thousands of years in the future? Oh, I would love to trade places with you! And I could, if you agreed."

"I don't think I understand," you reply.

"We can exchange lives," Hermes explains. "You'll become a god, and I'll go into the future and take your place."

"But you don't look like me. My family will know you're not me."

"We'll step into each other's bodies, too. Only you'll step into an immortal body," says Hermes. "Unfortunately, since you weren't born a god, you'll have all our powers except time travel."

Imagine *being* a god! That would be a thousand times better than just meeting one! But what about your family and friends?

If you say, "I'd rather just meet Zeus and then go home," turn to page 34.

If you agree to exchange lives with Hermes, turn to page 47.

Walking through the dark and barren halls of Hades's palace, you feel scared, but also sad and very lonely. There are no people, no doorways, no rays of sunlight. You are so relieved when you finally reach a shiny crimson door that you do not think twice about opening it.

Immediately, you wish you'd been more cautious. Three hideous old women with snakes for hair greet you with outstretched arms. You let out a blood-curdling scream and shut your eyes, but the gruesome sight burns into your mind.

A surprisingly gentle voice says, "Have no fear, young traveler. You may know us as the 'Furies,' but we stand for fairness, not just for rage."

Although you open your eyes, you still cannot bring yourself to look at the three women.

"We want to help you," says another of the Furies. "You don't belong in the Underworld, and it is not fair of Hades to keep you here."

"I just wanted to meet Zeus," you explain, stealing a glance at the Furies. You describe your parents' archaeological discovery and the troubles they've been facing. "I have to find a way for them to prove they've found Olympus."

The three Furies look at each other and smile. Suddenly, they begin to fly around you with such speed that they are transformed into a dark whirlwind. It is perfectly calm in the center of the tornado, where you stand, and you feel yourself slowly rising into the air. You lose track of everything except the black wind that surrounds you.

Turn to page 27.

24

You, Daedalus, and Icarus sit in the Labyrinth in silence. After a few hours, you begin to wonder if Athena has abandoned you. You think about dying and imagine floating past the walls of the Labyrinth and beyond.

"That's it!" you shout, jumping to your feet. "The way out of here is up!"

"And what do you suggest we do...*fly?*" Daedalus asks sarcastically, rolling his eyes.

"We won't fly, we'll walk," you tell him. "If Icarus climbs on your shoulders and I climb on top of his, I should be able to reach the top of these walls. Once I'm on top, I'll be able to see a way out and I'll lead you."

Icarus slaps you on the back. "I knew you'd save us!"

You wait until twilight so you will be less visible. Then you climb on top of Icarus and Daedalus, falling off a couple of times before managing to hoist yourself to the top of the wall. You survey the maze. Within minutes, you find a way to reach the entrance to the Labyrinth. Balancing carefully, you walk along the top of the walls as Icarus and Daedalus follow below.

Turn to page 26.

When at last you leave the maze, you hug each other jubilantly.

"I know some caves on the coast where we can hide until we figure out a way to escape from this island," says Daedalus. "You're welcome to come with us—or you can visit the palace of King Minos right over there. Minos may know how to find Zeus."

If you head towards the palace,
turn to page 36.

If you go with Icarus and Daedalus,
turn to page 51.

The next thing you know, you're back in Athens, in your own bed. The morning light is streaming through the windows and your father is shaking you.

"Wake up!" he exclaims. "Your mother and I are going back to the excavation. Last night I dreamed we unearthed all kinds of new evidence underneath the throne of Zeus. I know it sounds crazy, but in my dream, a black tornado drilled into the ground there, revealing crowns, ancient tablets—everything we need to prove our theory!"

"I dreamed about a black tornado, too," you say as you rub your eyes.

"How interesting," replies your father, but you can tell he's not really listening. Before you can say anything else, he leaves your room. You hear him hurry down the hall.

Sure enough, your parents discover more than enough evidence to prove that they found Olympus. And the day the famous Olympian artifacts first appear in the museum in Athens, a black tornado whips through the center of the city. The whirlwind creates much fear and commotion, but it causes no destruction at all.

The End

28

The Minotaur slowly extends his hand to grasp yours. The beast is trembling just as much as you are.

"You are the first person who has not run away from me," whispers the Minotaur hoarsely. Although his ability to speak astonishes you, you remind yourself that the Minotaur is part human.

"Maybe we can help each other escape," you suggest. "I imagine you'd rather not spend the rest of your life in this maze."

"I discovered the way out years ago, but I can't live outside it ever again. King Minos will search me out, and people are too afraid of me to help me hide. They know I eat human flesh."

A shiver runs up your spine. "You do?"

"Don't worry, I'd rather eat grass," the Minotaur assures you. "But all the king feeds me are his prisoners."

"I'm trying to find Zeus," you explain. "Why don't you come with me? We can ask him to transform you into a normal person."

"I'll show you the way out if you promise to stay with me once we leave the Labyrinth," says the Minotaur shyly.

Turn to page 31.

From the Shrine of Artemis, you gaze, transfixed, at the light inside the Parthenon. You are so mesmerized that you fail to notice another light moving toward you until it beams directly on your face.

You are blinded.

"Zeus?" you call expectantly.

"Stay where you are!" answers a voice that sounds very human and unmistakably angry. Before you can run, the watchman grabs your arm roughly and drags you away from the shrine.

From the guards' office, he phones the police. You remember this summer solstice for the rest of your life, although not for the reasons you had in mind.

The End

30

You turn and run. The Minotaur lunges after you as you race through the Labyrinth. The blood pounding in your ears muffles the sound of the beast's ferocious roars. Even though you run more swiftly than you ever thought possible, this is not a race you are destined to win.

The End

You briefly think about rescuing Icarus and Daedalus, but decide to escape immediately. Within minutes, you and the Minotaur are free.

"We'll have to leave the island or the king is sure to find me," he tells you as he scans the horizon. "As I recall, the harbor is in that direction. Maybe we can escape on a boat."

You leap onto the Minotaur's back, and together you race to the harbor. You see sailors loading cargo onto a boat and consider asking if they'll take you and the Minotaur on board. You doubt they'll greet the Minotaur warmly. You could try to sneak aboard and hide instead, but concealing your new friend won't be easy.

If you decide to explain your situation to the sailors, turn to page 49.

If you decide to hide with the Minotaur, turn to page 83.

It may be safer to stay in Hades's chariot—wherever it's taking you.

The chariot lands smoothly on the other side of the river. In a few minutes you arrive at a somber palace surrounded by high walls. The strangest creature you've ever seen waits by the gate. It is a gigantic dog, much bigger than you are, with three heads. He trots over to the chariot and frolics alongside.

"This is my dog, Cerberus," Hades explains. "He is always friendly when someone enters my kingdom. I must warn you, however, that if you attempt to leave my land, Cerberus will chew you to the bone." You smile weakly and pat one of the dog's heads. Cerberus licks your hand with an unnaturally cold tongue.

Hades leads you and Persephone down a gloomy hall to a pair of black marble thrones. "You will be my queen here forever, Persephone," says Hades as he gestures gallantly to the thrones, "so banish all memories of the Land of the Living." Nodding toward you, Hades remarks, "You, too, will remain in my kingdom for all eternity."

Turn to page 39.

"Well, I'm disappointed you won't trade lives with me," says Hermes, "but I'll take you as close to Olympus as I can. Zeus is very particular when it comes to mortal visitors, so I'll have to see if I can get an invitation for you."

You ride through groves of silvery trees, past orchards and villages, over the steepest mountains in Greece to a small peninsula. "Wait here," he tells you.

Moments later, he returns with Athena and Zeus. "Welcome to Olympus!" says Zeus cordially. You can't take your eyes off his robe. It seems to be woven of rainbows and lightning.

"Your grandmother and I are old friends," Zeus continues. "I look forward to talking with you. But let's have a bite to eat first."

Turn to page 42.

36

You say goodbye to Daedalus and Icarus and head for Minos's palace. From outside, the palace is not nearly as impressive as you thought it would be. Inside, however, the walls are vividly painted with large scenes of acrobats, dolphins, and monkeys. You wander through the brightly decorated corridors, occasionally poking your head into the rooms you pass.

In one room, you spot a pile of coarsely woven tunics. To avoid arousing suspicion, you substitute a tunic for your own clothing and hide your things at the bottom of the pile of tunics.

Feeling more confident now that you are well disguised, you ask the first servant you see to lead you to the king.

Go on to the next page.

The stone benches along the walls of the throne room are filled with people. Minos sits on a special throne, also carved of stone. It looks a little like the throne of Zeus your parents discovered, but it's much smaller. Kneeling before Minos, you introduce yourself and ask, "May I become your servant?"

"Even the most stupid person in Crete knows the king should not be approached so boldly," says Minos scornfully. "I could have you killed for such impudence! Where are you from?"

Turn to the next page.

You pause as you struggle to decide how to respond. He might be impressed if you tell him Athena brought you to Crete, but on the other hand, he might think you are lying.

If you say, "Athena brought me here so I could look for Zeus," turn to page 43.

If you reply, "I am an orphan from the other side of the island," turn to page 69.

Persephone sits down silently on the throne, staring blankly into space. You don't understand what has come over her, but it's clear that she won't be able to help you escape.

You're determined not to spend the rest of your life in the Underworld, though. "I'm going to explore the palace," you announce with false cheerfulness.

You wonder whether you should try to sneak past Cerberus or look for another escape route. Cerberus is certainly a frightening obstacle, but who knows what other terrors stand between you and the Land of the Living?

If you try your luck with Cerberus,
turn to page 12.

If you search for another way out of the palace,
turn to page 23.

40

Slowly you circle the Parthenon, waiting for the crowd to thin out. When it does, you quickly scramble over the fence, run up the stairs to the temple, and hide behind an immense column. You wait nervously as the shadows grow longer. You listen to the guards making their rounds, and your heart beats so loudly you feel certain they will hear it. Finally the sky darkens and the first stars begin to appear.

"Oh, please," you wish out loud, "let me meet Zeus. No one wants to meet him more than I do." No sooner do the words leave your lips than a small white spark flashes next to you. At first you think it's a firefly, but then you notice five, six, seven sparks bursting like popcorn.

As the tiny flashes continue, you hold your breath with fear and fascination. Then, to your amazement, the sparks form into a tall and graceful woman wearing white robes.

Turn to page 18.

42

Zeus leads you to an enormous table surrounded by immense thrones. You gaze in awe at the gods and goddesses gathered around the table. You imagined they would be dignified, but instead they tease one another and laugh so hard the table trembles. Zeus creates a small cloud for your seat, and you sit down to enjoy the meal.

When the last morsel of food has been devoured, Zeus takes you aside. "I have a souvenir for you," he says, handing you a shovel made of mirrors. "If you use this shovel, you will be able to unearth every last trace of Olympus. Just follow the tug of this tool and you will find more than you have ever dreamed of."

You thank Zeus and return to your cloud seat. When you sit, however, you discover it is no longer firm.... You sink into silvery vapors and tumble through time.

When the mists clear, you find yourself at home, still clutching your souvenir from Zeus.

The End

Minos raises his eyebrows. "Athena brought you here? What business do you have with Zeus?"

"I live thousands of years in the future," you say. "My parents are trying to prove they've discovered Olympus, but everyone thinks they're crazy. I came to get help from Zeus."

Nervous laughter fills the room, but Minos ignores it. He leans forward and eyes you intently. "Tell me about life in the future."

"Well," you pause, wondering where to begin, "we have machines that carry people through the air. We also have machines that carry people over land. They're a little like chariots, I guess, but they don't need horses for power. We have rockets that travel through outer space, and people have even walked on the moon."

"Humans have stepped on the moon?" asks Minos, incredulously.

"Yes," you assure him, "and we've sent spaceships to Mars and Saturn."

"This is fascinating!" says Minos. "Never mind about becoming a servant. I want to hear more about the future. Your knowledge will help my kingdom prosper."

You spend the rest of your life at the palace of Minos. Under your guidance, Crete becomes an unusually advanced civilization. You're proud of your contribution, but sometimes you awake in the middle of the night and wonder why Athena abandoned you and if your parents were ever able to prove their archaeological discovery.

The End

44

You throw two branches close to each other. Cerberus catches each of the limbs in a different mouth. Then you throw three branches, still very close together. Cerberus eagerly retrieves them.

Finally, mustering up all your strength, you fling three branches as far as you can, but each in a different direction. One of Cerberus's heads spots the first limb and sets off after it. The second and third heads strain as they struggle to go in other directions. One head snarls at another and nips the third one. Suddenly all three heads are fighting!

Wasting no time, you slip through the gate. Even though you're not sure where you are going, you run as fast as you can away from the palace. Before long, you reach the river Styx. You are surprised to see an old man in a hooded cloak guiding a boat across the river. When he notices you, he waves and approaches the shore.

Turn to page 52.

"I'll trade lives with you on one condition," you tell Hermes. "You must promise to help my parents prove they've discovered Olympus."

Hermes grins. "I know where Zeus keeps all his treasures. I'll make your parents famous."

Hermes places his hand gently over your face and tells you to do the same to him. A throbbing pulse, much stronger than a heartbeat, fills your body. Hermes removes his hand from your face and says, "Now take your hand away."

You are startled beyond words to see your own face and clothing on someone else. Hermes's entire body has changed into your own! You realize you're wearing his robe and winged sandals.

Suddenly panic seizes you. "How will I know how to be a god? How will I recognize the other gods?"

"Don't worry," Hermes replies. "You'll recognize Zeus the same way I'll recognize your parents, because we've added each other's knowledge and experiences to our own."

Sure enough, you realize you do know exactly what Zeus looks like. You even know where to find him. You hug Hermes—now yourself—goodbye. With the last of his godly powers, Hermes whisks himself through time.

You begin to run toward Olympus. Your body feels weightless, and your feet barely touch the ground. When you finally see the splendor of Olympus, there is no doubt in your mind that you're going to like being a god!

The End

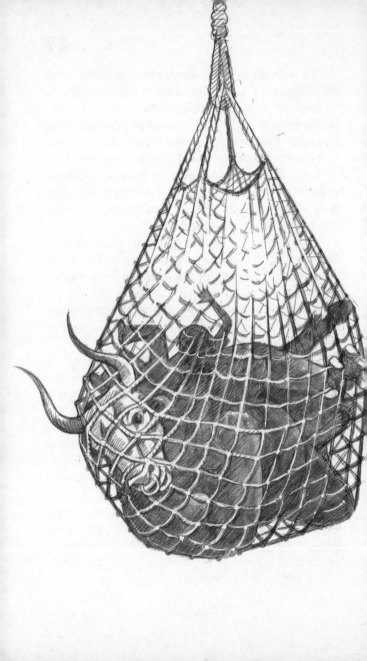

"Hello!" you call as you climb aboard the boat. The Minotaur trails behind you uneasily.

A sailor turns to answer you, but before the words leave his lips, he spots the Minotaur and screams. The next thing you know, you and the Minotaur are trapped under a fishing net.

"I just wanted to ask a favor," you cry as you struggle to free yourself from the heavy net. The sailors ignore your pleas as they gather the net tightly around you both and secure it with ropes.

The sailors congratulate themselves. "King Minos is sure to reward us generously for catching the Minotaur and its accomplice!" one exclaims gleefully.

As you wait for the king's arrival, you know you are doomed.

The End

50

With Daedalus, you travel by boat to Athens. You want to begin your search for Zeus as soon as you arrive, but Daedalus disagrees. "You can't look for Zeus the same way you might look for a friend in the marketplace! You must attract Zeus to you. If you become my apprentice, I'll teach you to be such a clever craftsman that Zeus will surely take notice of you."

You consent. Daedalus shows you how to make magical things—wooden flutes that play the songs of nightingales, clay urns that never run out of water, and special nets that turn fish into pearls.

At first, you awaken each day with the hope that Zeus will visit you. But as the years pass, and your work becomes even more wondrous, you forget about Zeus, and even your family. After all, you are so talented that even Periphas, the king of Athens, buys a flute from you.

The End

All through the night, the three of you trudge across the island toward the caves. You climb treacherously rocky hills and pass olive trees that glimmer like silver in the moonlight, but you are so troubled by a vague worry that you pay little attention to the scenery. Near dawn, you reach the caves. Resting against a cool stone, you fall into a fitful sleep.

A few hours later, you awake with a distressing realization. You remember that your grandmother used to tell you a story about Icarus and Daedalus when you were younger. In the legend, they used special wings to fly away from Crete. The part when Icarus falls into the sea and drowns always made you so sad that your grandmother finally stopped telling you the tale.

Maybe it's not a true story, you think. But what if it is? As you stumble out of the cave, you decide to speak to Daedalus about your fears.

Turn to page 54.

"I don't remember meeting you before," says the old man as he pulls his raft ashore, "but I suppose I must have. I've been at this job since the beginning of time, and it's getting to be too much for me."

"I don't think we've met," you reply, extending your hand and introducing yourself. "Who are you?"

"Charon, ferryman of the dead," he answers wearily.

"Well, I'm trying to reach the Land of the Living," you explain.

Charon laughs scornfully. "You and millions of others. I can't help you. The passengers I carry go only in one direction—toward Hades."

"But I'm not dead!" you exclaim impatiently. "I don't belong in the Underworld."

"None of the inhabitants of the Underworld believe they belong here," says Charon. "I'll admit, though, that you do have a certain vitality I don't see very often around here. And where did you get such unusual clothing?"

"In the twenty-first century, where I come from, these are very normal clothes. You see, I'm just visiting your time. I need to get on with my search for Zeus."

Go on to the next page.

Charon laughs. "You're pretty amusing. How would you like to become my apprentice? I'd welcome a joke every now and then."

"I would bring dead people across the river on your boat?" you ask. The idea of transporting bodies makes your skin crawl.

"Under my close supervision," answers Charon. "Don't worry, it's not unpleasant work. The passengers are souls, not reeking corpses."

Working for Charon might offer the best chance for escape from the Underworld, but you wonder how long you would have to wait for the right moment. Should you try to swim across the river Styx on your own?

If you decide to swim, turn to page 82.

If you agree to become Charon's apprentice, turn to page 93.

54

You find Icarus and Daedalus constructing large wings just outside the cave. They sew the long feathers together and bind the smaller ones with beeswax. Smiling at you, Icarus says, "Your idea of looking upward for escape inspired my father. We're going to fly off this island!"

Your stomach sinks.

"I don't think that's a good idea," you stammer.

"And why not?" asks Daedalus, not looking up from his work.

"Something bad will happen. I just know it will," you insist.

"Nonsense!" snorts Daedalus. He grabs your arm and yanks you into the cave. "I don't want you putting ideas in Icarus's head!" he snaps. "Just because you figured out a way to escape from the Labyrinth, don't think you're the only one with good ideas. Let me tell you something—all through Greece I'm known for my clever schemes."

"People in my country speak of your inventions, too," you reply. "We tell a story about the wings you are building. In the story, the beeswax melts when Icarus flies too close to the sun. He drowns."

Turn to page 58.

You decide not to try to escape. When Poseidon returns, he announces that he's meeting with Zeus to discuss the hurricane.

"Come with me to Olympus," Poseidon tells you, "but be careful to wash only the prettiest shells onto the beach. The gods hate having their shoreline littered with dead fish and seaweed."

You work obediently while the gods talk business. As Zeus begins to walk toward the water's edge to say goodbye to Poseidon, you fling an array of the most exquisite shells in the underwater kingdom onto the beach. Zeus kneels in the foam to examine the rare shells. When the next wave washes onto the shore, you glide with it and wrap your arms tightly around Zeus's ankles.

You feel the cold grasp of Poseidon around your legs and plead, "Help me, Zeus!"

Zeus orders Poseidon to release you and pulls you out of the water. "You're a mortal being, not a water nymph!" he exclaims. "No wonder you want to escape from Poseidon!"

Turn to page 59.

56

"Give me an arrow!" Hercules bellows, but you ignore him. He sneers as the Daughters of the Evening Land embrace you.

"I'll show you I don't need the help of a pipsqueak! I can tear this dragon to shreds with my bare hands!"

You watch Hercules wrestle with the beast. Each time the dragon snaps at Hercules, he yells with surprise, and you're smugly pleased to see him struggle. Only when the dragon finally chases Hercules away does a quiet peace descend over the garden.

"He'll be back," you tell the Daughters. "He doesn't give up."

"We know," one replies, "but at least we'll have one more evening."

"Now dream," another whispers. You feel yourself drifting into a delightful sleep.

When you awake, you are in your own bed in Athens. You have no memory of your ancient adventures. You can't remember how you got home from the Acropolis, but a dream about meeting Athena lingers faintly in your mind. As you climb out of bed, you notice a golden apple beside your pillow.

You spend the rest of your life wondering where that apple came from.

The End

"Quick!" you cry. "Into the caves!"

You and Icarus run into the caverns and crawl through serpentine tunnels. After several hours of waiting, you are convinced you've eluded Daedalus. You are eager to leave the damp darkness of the caves.

When you finally emerge, you see a bearded man in a robe that seems to have been woven of rainbows and sunlight. Turning to you, he says, "I am Zeus. Remember, you are mortal." Before you can respond, he continues, "I control mortal fates and you do not. I understand why you wanted to prevent the death of your friend Icarus, but life and death are my responsibilities. I do not welcome interference."

"I'm sorry," you whisper, although you really aren't at all sorry.

"What do you think I should do with Icarus? I have not planned anything—a marriage, children, even a job—for his future," Zeus muses.

Icarus bites his lip in terror.

"Send him home with me to the twenty-first century!" you suggest.

Zeus is silent for a moment, then grins. "That's a fine idea! His presence should stir up a lot of excitement in your century."

Icarus drops to his knees and murmurs, "Thank you, great Zeus!"

Turn to page 108.

58

"Where do you come from?" asks Daedalus. "Do you mean to tell me that everyone in your country tells stories about things that haven't even happened yet?"

"I live in Athens, but thousands of years in the future," you explain. "We call what you are doing now 'ancient history.'"

Daedalus laughs. "I thought you were jealous, but now I see that you're just crazy. But don't worry, I'll tell Icarus not to fly too high. And," he adds, winking as he pats your shoulder, "you'd better not fly too high, yourself."

If you try to persuade Icarus not to fly, turn to page 65.

If you decide you've had enough of Daedalus and want to concentrate on finding Zeus, turn to page 106.

You tell Zeus about your adventures in ancient Greece and explain your parents' archaeological project. "Please tell me how I can help them prove they've found the real Olympus."

"I'd be happy to assist such a worthy endeavor," Zeus replies. He picks up a shell and clenches it tightly. When he gives it to you, you see that the shell has turned to gold. It pulses gently in your hand.

"Just concentrate and this shell will lead you to whatever you seek," says Zeus.

"That's terrific! Thanks so much!" you exclaim. "But how do I return to the twenty-first century?"

Zeus smiles and points to the shell. "Close your eyes and think of something you want to find. Imagine a chair in your home, for instance."

When you open your eyes, you are sitting in your rocking chair, holding the magic shell.

The End

60

He thanks you profusely. "I slipped into the gully two days ago," he explains, "and I was beginning to think I'd never get out. If you come with me to my father's palace, I'm sure he'll reward you for saving my life."

"Is King Minos your father?"

"No, my father is the god of the sun, Helios, and I'm Phaeton."

"You're kidding! Does your father live on Olympus?"

"I don't think so," answers Phaeton. "My mother said he lives in the Palace of the Sun."

"You mean you're not sure?"

"Well, I haven't seen him in a long time. A lot of my friends don't believe Helios is my father. I'm going to *prove* that he is by driving the Chariot of the Sun," says Phaeton.

Your heart pounds with excitement as you imagine driving the chariot that brings daylight to the earth.

"Do you want to come with me?" Phaeton asks.

"Sure!" you reply, and the two of you set off for the Palace of the Sun.

Turn to page 63.

"I'll come with you," you say to Hercules, and you tie up the Bull of Minos.

You follow Hercules to a wide pasture filled with red cattle. As you help round up the herd, a two-headed dog springs onto your back, knocking you to the ground. It is as big as a small car—so big that it could easily smother you. When it bares its teeth in a ferocious snarl, dark foam drips from its jaws. You struggle to scream, but even your vocal cords are paralyzed with fear.

Suddenly you hear the sound of crunching bone as Hercules smashes both of the dog's fierce heads. He carries it to the top of a nearby hill and hurls the body into the sea. You try to catch your breath and rise to your feet. Your heart is still pounding uncontrollably when you see Geryon, an immense monster with three heads attached to one grotesque body, grab Hercules from behind.

As you watch Hercules grapple with the monster, you realize how fierce an opponent Geryon is— even for a hero as powerful as Hercules. You're determined to help Hercules, but how?

If you try to distract the monster by running close to it, turn to page 66.

If you decide to throw rocks at the monster, turn to page 86.

As you walk with Phaeton through the night, he talks about driving the Chariot of the Sun and you explain your search for Zeus. When you notice light glowing on the horizon, you point out the sunrise to Phaeton.

"It's not dawn yet," he answers. "I think that is the light of my father's palace."

As you approach the palace, you wish you had sunglasses. Even when you squint your eyes, the light is dazzling. You can barely see that the palace is made of jewels and ivory. Inside, the light is blinding. You cover your eyes with your hands and peer through the space between your fingers.

"Phaeton! What brings you to my palace?" a kind voice asks.

"Father?"

"Yes, it's me," Helios says. "I'll take off my crown of light so you'll be able to see me."

Turn to the next page.

Your eyes stop burning and you open them cautiously. Although the light is still bright, you can see a tall man dressed in golden armor. Phaeton introduces you and describes how you rescued him. Then he complains that his friends don't believe he is the son of a god.

"As proof that I am your father," says Helios, "I will grant you anything you desire."

Phaeton does not hesitate. "There is only one thing I want. Just once, let me drive your chariot across the sky."

Turn to page 67.

Later in the day, you approach Icarus while he is gathering feathers on a nearby hillside. He waves and exclaims, "I can't wait to fly!"

"Icarus, we can't fly," you pant as you stumble toward him. "It's too dangerous. We'll die!" As the words leave your lips, you suddenly wonder whether or not you are destined to survive the flight.

"Don't be afraid," says Icarus kindly. "My father is brilliant. None of his inventions has ever failed."

"This one is destined to fail," you retort. A new idea occurs to you, and you tell him, "I've been warned by the gods that you will fly so close to the sun that the wax in your wings will melt. You'll fall to the sea and drown!"

Icarus is silent for a moment, then says solemnly, "Is that why Athena sent you here?"

"Yes," you nod. You feel a bit guilty for lying, but you remind yourself that perhaps Athena *does* want you to save Icarus.

"I still want to fly," Icarus replies, "but I promise I'll fly below you the entire time. I'll stay as far from the sun as you like. Is that all right?"

If you agree, turn to page 72.

If you can't bring yourself to go along with this plan, and instead say goodbye to Icarus and Daedalus, turn to page 106.

66

Mustering all your courage, you race up the hill where Hercules and Geryon are fighting. Standing only a few feet from the monster, you wave your arms and jump around to catch its attention. Sure enough, Geryon turns its enormous heads toward you.

One of the monster's hairy arms yanks you off your feet. Geryon stumbles away from Hercules, gripping you tightly. The monster dashes into a cave at the bottom of the hill.

Hercules runs after you, but not quickly enough. By the time he reaches the cave, you have already become Geryon's lunch.

The End

"Not even Zeus can drive my chariot!" Helios exclaims with horror. "I doubt a mortal being could survive the journey! Please, Phaeton, reconsider your request while I reward your friend." Helios turns to you. "I owe you Phaeton's life. I will give you anything."

You desperately want to drive the Chariot of the Sun, but Helios's warning makes you wonder if instead you should ask him to introduce you to Zeus.

If you say, "I would like to meet Zeus,"
turn to page 94.

If you're determined to drive the Chariot of the Sun, turn to page 120.

"There is no one in your village who can care for you?" asks Minos with surprising sympathy.

"No," you reply solemnly.

"Theo," Minos calls to one of his attendants. "Train this orphan to tend the cows."

You work very hard, feeding and milking the royal herd. One day, Theo announces that he wants you to guard the Bull of Minos.

"It is a sacred beast, a gift from the god Poseidon," Theo explains. "It is hidden in the hills. Only a few of us know the location."

The Bull of Minos is an enormous white creature that barely takes notice of you. With two other servants, you take turns guarding it.

One day, as you walk to the pen to begin your shift of guard duty, a large man wearing a leopard skin approaches you. You can't take your eyes off the massive muscles that ripple with every move he makes.

"My name is Hercules," he says quietly. "Maybe you've heard of me."

Of course you've heard of Hercules! This is almost as exciting as meeting Zeus!

"I'm trying to find the Bull of Minos," Hercules explains.

"Why?" you ask.

Hercules sighs. "A few years ago, I went insane. In a fit of rage, I killed my wife and children. As punishment, the king of Mycenae has given me twelve labors to perform. They are very arduous. For one of the labors, I have to steal the Bull of Minos."

Turn to page 74.

70

You lead Hercules to the Bull of Minos. With just the slightest struggle, Hercules grabs the bull by its horns and flings the animal over his shoulders.

"Come on," he tells you. "We're going to the island of Erytheia next."

"Do you think Zeus will be there?" you ask hopefully.

Hercules shrugs. "All I know is I have to get red cattle from Geryon. Between the monster Geryon and its two-headed dog, Orthus, this is going to be a tough labor."

At the mention of the word "monster," you realize just how dangerous the next task will be. You're not happy, but you say nothing.

You sail to Erytheia, the Red Isle, with Hercules and the bull in a giant golden cup. It's like a boat, except that it has no sail and seems to move wherever Hercules wants. When you reach the island, Hercules pulls the golden cup ashore and proceeds to yank a full-grown tree out of the ground.

"This tree will make a great weapon," he says, noting your gaze. "Do you want to help me with this battle or guard the bull?"

The battle promises to be more exciting, but also dangerous. Guarding the bull would be safe… unless Geryon spots and attacks you before it sees Hercules!

If you follow Hercules into the hills of Erytheia,
turn to page 61.

If you volunteer to watch the Bull of Minos,
turn to page 81.

You and Icarus spend the next few days gathering feathers while Daedalus fashions three pairs of wings. Icarus talks constantly about flying, while you quietly ponder your fate. How can you be sure your wings will survive the fierce heat of the sun?

Daedalus ties them to your arms and explains how they work. "Just remember," he teases, "don't fly too close to the sun."

Icarus catches your eye. "We won't," you reply in unison.

You walk to a cliff overlooking the sea. Daedalus takes a running leap over the edge. Frantically flapping his wings, he manages to fly. It's your turn next, and you say goodbye to Icarus.

As you run to the edge of the cliff, you're so terrified you can hardly breathe.

If you continue running, determined to fly, turn to page 80.

If you decide you'd rather not risk your life in flight, turn to page 92.

"Why should I show you where the bull is?" you ask. "I'll only get myself into trouble."

"Maybe I can do you a favor in exchange," Hercules says.

"Maybe," you agree. You explain your quest and ask, "Could you help me find Zeus?"

"Zeus is my father, so I do see him every now and then," replies Hercules, "but first, I have to finish the twelve labors."

You are afraid of what Hercules might do to you if you don't let him steal the bull. Yet you know King Minos well enough to worry about what he'll do when he learns you betrayed him. And who knows how long it will take Hercules to accomplish the remaining labors before he can introduce you to Zeus?

If you refuse to help Hercules at all,
turn to page 19.

If you agree to show Hercules the Bull of Minos
in exchange for his help in finding Zeus,
turn to page 70.

After Daedalus leaves, you spend a few days exploring Icaria. But Zeus is nowhere to be found. Each time you pass Icarus's grave, you're overwhelmed with sorrowful memories. Finally you decide to continue your search in another part of Greece.

Maybe working on a boat will offer you a chance to seek Zeus in new lands. You wait at the harbor until a ship docks, then ask the captain if you may join his crew. He welcomes you warmly, but a sly glint in his eyes makes you nervous. Although he doesn't ask you about what you're wearing, he offers you a new set of clothes.

While some of the sailors show you around the ship and explain the work, an older teenage boy comes aboard. He is exceptionally handsome, and his clothing is very fine. "My name is Dionysus. I will pay you to take me to the island of Naxos," he says to the crew. The captain agrees eagerly, and the ship sets sail.

Although you are glad to leave Icaria, a sixth sense warns you that something is wrong. During the night, your suspicions are confirmed when you overhear a conversation between two sailors.

Turn to page 77.

"I don't like the captain's order to kidnap the rich boy," mutters one.

"You will, you will," replies the second sailor. "Once we have the ransom, you'll be glad we have such an enterprising leader."

Kidnap Dionysus! You wonder what the captain plans to do with you! Casually—although your heart is pounding fiercely—you stroll away from the sailors and explore the deck.

Sure enough, you spot Dionysus bound to a mast and gagged. Three oarsmen guard him, but none of them see you. You wonder what you should do.

If you decide to mind your own business and stay out of trouble, turn to page 96.

If you are determined to help Dionysus, turn to page 100.

You take a deep breath and hurl yourself out of Hades's chariot.

The icy waters of the river Styx swallow you. By the time you struggle to the surface, Persephone and Hades have disappeared. You begin swimming to the shore, but you feel dangerously weak. Each stroke of your arms seems to require more strength than you can muster. Your body feels terribly heavy as the river Styx drags you into its murky depths.

The End

"What is the name of the island?" you ask Athena as she carries you toward it.

"Until today, it had no name," she answers, "but from now on, it will be called Icaria in honor of your friend."

Athena deposits you on the coast of the island. Before you can ask her any more questions, she disappears abruptly. You look around anxiously, trying to understand how she left so quickly, but all you can see is Daedalus swimming to shore with the body of Icarus. The boy's limbs, as well as his wings, are broken. His head hangs lifelessly toward his chest. You feel so sad that you wonder if it was a mistake to come to Icaria.

"I'm so sorry," you stammer uncomfortably.

"Don't apologize," Daedalus replies woefully. "You warned me and I ignored you. It's all my fault."

You help Daedalus bury his son and try your best to comfort him. You remind him that you need to find Zeus.

"Well, come to Athens with me," suggests Daedalus.

"Have you ever seen Zeus in Athens?"

"No," Daedalus replies, "but the most exciting things happen in Athens, so I'm sure Zeus must visit frequently."

If you decide to join Daedalus, turn to page 50.

If you decide to make sure Zeus isn't on Icaria, turn to page 75.

80

You close your eyes and jump off the cliff. You catch a gulp of air and beat your wings with all your might, but continue to fall. It isn't until you are within a few feet of the sea that your descent slows and you begin to fly upward. The wings work!

Flapping harder, you soar into the sky. You glance over your shoulder and see Icarus fluttering safely behind you. You slow your flight until he is directly below you.

"Don't worry," he calls. "I'll stay with you."

As your confidence grows, you experiment with a few daring swoops. You try flying figure eights. Icarus mimics all your motions, and together you travel far from the island of Crete.

When you look toward the sun to check your distance, you notice a woman in white robes flying above you! When she calls your name, you realize that it's Athena. She motions for you to join her—and forgetting Icarus, you soar higher.

You are still far from Athena when you begin to feel heat on your back. The light is so bright that you have to squint. You remember Icarus and look for him. To your horror, he is flying just below you! Before you have a chance to say anything, you notice feathers fluttering off his wings.

You look at your own wings with alarm. Droplets of wax are sliding along the larger feathers, and many small feathers have come loose!

Just then, you feel yourself starting to sink.

Turn to page 84.

Hercules waves goodbye as he sets off to steal the red cattle. You feed the Bull of Minos some grass, then decide to go for a swim. The water is so warm and calm that you relax despite yourself. You float near the shore and gaze at the cloudless sky.

Suddenly a cold rush of water envelops your body, gripping you tightly. An unseen force drags you underwater and pulls you farther from shore. At first you're sure you're drowning, but then you realize you are able to breathe underwater. This discovery makes you only a little less frightened.

As your eyes adjust to the salty water, you see a large human shape that seems to be made of nothing more than thousands of dark green whirlpools.

"I gave that bull to Minos!" the creature roars.

"Who are you?" you ask. Water rushes into your mouth and fills your lungs.

"Poseidon, god of the oceans."

"Well, I'm sorry about the bull," you stammer.

"I don't want apologies, I want revenge," Poseidon bellows. "Help me trap Hercules and I'll let you go. Otherwise, I'll keep you here forever."

You hate the idea of spending the rest of your life underwater with Poseidon, but you'd feel awful about betraying Hercules.

If you refuse to help Poseidon,
turn to page 115.

If you agree to lure Hercules into the ocean,
turn to page 124.

"Thanks," you tell Charon, "but if you won't carry me across the river, I'll just swim."

Charon laughs devilishly. "So many souls have attempted the same folly."

You hesitate and survey the river more carefully. It is not very wide, and the current isn't swift. You decide to ignore Charon's comment and step into the icy water. He makes no attempt to stop you.

As you swim through the shimmering waves, you feel your strength ebbing away. By the time you reach the opposite shore, you are too weak even to stand. You are, in fact, lifeless.

Charon floats across the river and lifts your limp body onto his boat. "No one survives the river Styx," mutters Charon. "Just one more soul to carry across the water."

You spend eternity in the Underworld.

The End

When no one is watching, you and the Minotaur board the boat and hide below deck. You wedge yourself between sacks of grain and the Minotaur crouches nearby among crates of clucking chickens.

You have barely settled into place when the Minotaur loudly exclaims, "The boat is leaving the dock!"

"Quiet!" you whisper. "We can't say a word, or they'll hear us!"

The sea becomes frightfully turbulent during the night. Thunder rumbles and the chickens squawk. The boat lurches from side to side. You hear water rush along the deck, and the Minotaur moans beside you.

Maybe you should climb above to see what's happening on deck. You want to know how serious the storm is, but is it worth the risk that one of the sailors might see you?

*If you make your way onto the deck,
turn to page 88.*

*If you stay with the Minotaur below deck,
turn to page 91.*

84

You crash into Icarus. A tangle of feathers, bodies, and sticky wax, the two of you plummet toward the sea with breathtaking speed. Suddenly you find yourself in Athena's arms. A second later, you hear the splash of Icarus hitting the water.

"We have to save him!" you cry. "It's all my fault!"

"You're not to blame," Athena explains. "Icarus had to die this way. None of us can change his fate. Now, tell me—shall I drop you off on that island over there, or do you want me to carry you over Greece for a while?"

If you've had enough of flying and ask Athena to carry you to the island, turn to page 79.

If you decide to survey ancient Greece from the air with Athena, go on to the next page.

You're sad about Icarus, but you do want to keep looking for Zeus.

"I'll come with you," you tell Athena. "Maybe we'll be able to see Zeus from here."

"I never promised you would meet him," she reminds you.

"I know. Could we just fly over Olympus so I can see his throne?"

Athena carries you over countless islands, past Athens, to a small peninsula. She points out a huge table with eleven wooden thrones. At the head of the table stands a large stone throne that looks just like the one your parents unearthed. You tell Athena about your parents' archaeological project.

"I wanted to ask Zeus how my parents could prove that they've found Olympus and not just another ancient throne," you explain.

"Why didn't you tell me all this before?" Athena exclaims. "I could have told you that Zeus keeps the Olympian Orders buried beneath his throne. Tell your parents to dig deeper and they'll have all the evidence they need." Then she twirls you around and sends you back home.

Sure enough, once you convince your parents, Athena's advice leads them to the most important archaeological discovery of the century. The next year, on the summer solstice, you go to the Parthenon to thank Athena. She never appears, but somehow you know she understands.

The End

Quickly you gather an armload of rocks and hide behind a bush. Taking careful aim, you hurl a stone at Geryon's back. The monster pauses and looks around, giving Hercules a chance to land a forceful punch in its nearest face. Your second stone hits Geryon directly in the eye, stunning it for a moment. Hercules knocks the monster to the ground and kills it with an arrow.

Hercules slaps you on the back and says, "I don't know if I could have won that battle without your help." Together, you lead the red cattle to the golden cup and set sail for Mycenae, where you will deliver the cattle before beginning the next labor.

When Hercules describes his next endeavor—stealing the golden apples from the Daughters of the Evening Land—you ask him if he ever feels guilty about stealing precious bulls and cattle and golden apples from their owners.

Hercules does not seem to understand. As the days pass, you feel increasingly uncomfortable about helping him with his next labor. You wonder if once you reach Mycenae you should stay there and continue your search for Zeus alone.

On the other hand, Hercules is one of Zeus's sons, so you may stand a better chance of meeting his father if you remain with him.

If you decide to say goodbye to Hercules in Mycenae, turn to page 113.

If you decide to accompany Hercules to the Daughters of the Evening Land, turn to page 117.

88

As you stumble onto the deck, a wave crashes into you, knocking you off your feet. Another wave washes you overboard.

You thrash around in the violent water and finally manage to grab a broad wooden plank. You crawl on top of it and hold on tightly. When you catch your breath enough to look around, you see that the boat has sunk! You search for a sign of the Minotaur and realize sadly that it has gone down with the ship.

The storm gradually passes. By morning the sea is almost calm. The waves gently carry you by a school of dolphins. They frolic so playfully that for a brief moment you forget the terror of the previous night.

One dolphin swims around you a few times, then floats beside you. You stroke its smooth back and suddenly wonder if you should climb on for a ride.

You have no idea how the dolphin will react; maybe you're safer staying on the plank. But if you do that, how long will you have to drift before someone rescues you?

If you remain floating on the wooden plank, turn to page 3.

If you climb onto the dolphin's back, go on to the next page.

Once you are on its back, the dolphin stops romping and soars through the sea with alarming speed. It seems to know exactly where it is going. When you approach a small peninsula, the dolphin glides onto a beach. You roll off its back and press your face into the sand. You're grateful to be on land again!

Turn to the next page.

Turning to the dolphin, you are astonished to see a large bearded man in its place. He wears a golden crown and a remarkable robe that looks as if it might have been woven from rainbows.

"You're lucky I felt like being a dolphin today," says the man, straightening his crown and smiling at your sandy face.

"What are you usually?" you ask, brushing the sand off your nose and forehead.

"Well, I'm always Zeus, but every now and then I like to experiment with a different body."

You are speechless.

"I've heard you've been looking for me," says Zeus.

You describe your parents' archaeological exploration and the troubles they face. Zeus listens intently. When you are finished, he wordlessly leads you to an immense table with twelve thrones. Eleven of them are elaborately carved from olive wood. The twelfth, which you recognize from your parents' photos, is stone.

Turn to page 98.

Despite your worries about the storm, you decide not to risk going on deck.

The Minotaur clutches your arm as the storm rages. The boat slowly fills with water. The crates of chickens smash together, and wet feathers float everywhere.

"Let's get out of here!" you shriek to the Minotaur above the deafening roar of thunder. You struggle to get out from under the sacks of grain, but it's too late. They are soaked with water and have become too heavy for even the Minotaur to budge.

Images of your family flash through your mind. You know you will never see them again. The last thing you hear is the Minotaur bellowing as the boat sinks into the churning sea.

The End

92

You come to an abrupt stop at the edge of the cliff. "I'm not going to fly," you tell Icarus as you struggle to catch your breath. "I don't want to die and I don't want to see you die."

Icarus is silent.

"Go ahead and fly if you want to," you say.

"I don't want to die either," he slowly answers, "but my father is going to be furious when he realizes we haven't followed him."

Sure enough, Daedalus is already flying toward you, shouting, "Come on! Flap those wings!"

"He's going to make me fly," says Icarus sorrowfully. "I just know it."

"Maybe together we can convince him that flying is just too dangerous," you suggest. "Or, if you don't think that will work, we could hide in the caves. He'll never be able to find us."

Icarus is trembling with fear. "I don't know what to do. You decide."

If you run into the caves, turn to page 57.

If you wait for Daedalus to land so you can talk with him, turn to page 95.

You step gingerly onto Charon's boat. He shows you how to guide it with a pole to the other side of the river where you wait for passengers.

The job is not as ghoulish as you had feared. Your passengers remind you of Persephone. They look like normal people, except that their faces are unnaturally pale and expressionless. They rarely speak. You avoid looking in their eyes.

Soon you realize it will not be as easy to escape as you had hoped. Charon never sleeps. He never lets you out of his sight. And whenever the boat approaches the shore, he holds on to your shoulders with such force that there is no way you can get away.

But as the weeks pass, Charon begins to trust you. He grips your shoulders less firmly. Finally he stops holding you altogether. Although you know you could probably escape now, you are troubled. Part of you wants to return immediately to the Land of the Living, but another part of you worries about Persephone. Do you dare return to the palace of Hades to rescue her?

If you decide to go directly to the Land of the Living, turn to page 101.

If you think you should help Persephone, turn to page 105.

"So you want to meet Zeus?" asks Helios. "I'll invite him right away. Please excuse me, but if you'll just wait here for Zeus, Phaeton and I are going to have a talk about his dangerous desire to drive my chariot."

Shortly after Helios and Phaeton leave, a lightning bolt flashes right inside the palace! A bearded man in a radiant, rainbow-colored robe stands before you.

"Zeus!" you gasp.

"Yes," he replies, "Helios asked if I would see you."

"I have a favor to ask," you explain as you begin to describe your parents' discovery of his throne.

"That's grand!" says Zeus gleefully. "I always hated the idea of my throne being buried underground for centuries. Let's surprise your parents! While they're still in Athens, you and I will go to Olympus and time-travel to the excavation. That way, I'll be able to show you exactly where my treasures are buried."

"Thanks so much!" you exclaim.

"Not at all," Zeus replies. "Now if we hurry, perhaps Helios can drop us off at Olympus while he drives his chariot across the sky."

The End

Daedalus lands awkwardly. His face is distorted with rage as he yells, "What's wrong with you two?"

"It's too dangerous!" you insist.

"I changed my mind. I don't want to fly," Icarus stammers.

"I don't care what happens to Athena's little friend," says Daedalus as he glares nastily in your direction, "but you're my son, Icarus, and you're going to fly!"

Daedalus drags Icarus to the cliff and shoves him over the edge. Desperately flapping his wings, Icarus manages to soar into the air. Without a word of farewell, Daedalus flies after his son, leaving you alone on the cliff.

You cannot bear to watch Icarus. Feeling very forlorn, you bury your face in your hands. When at last you lift your head, you discover there is a bearded man sitting beside you. You eye his delicate rainbow-colored robe in astonishment. "Zeus?" you whisper hesitantly.

Turn to page 112.

You decide to try and get some sleep, and you hide under a pile of fishy-smelling nets. Just before dawn, you awake. Ivy and grapevines are twined all over the masts, oars, and even the nets covering you. You hear flutes playing an eerie tune. You wonder if you're going crazy.

Your hair stands on end. Wild beasts—lions, panthers, and bears—are roaming the deck! You duck under the nets again. The animals' snarls punctuate the sailors' frightened screams.

You peer out from the nets and see the largest lion savagely mauling the captain while Dionysus calmly watches. You feel sick to your stomach.

A nearby sailor exclaims, "I knew this was the wrong boy to kidnap! He's no rich kid, he's a god!"

Before you have a chance to ask any questions, you notice a panther sniffing the nets just a few feet away from you. Without thinking twice, you leap out from under the nets and jump overboard.

Several sailors follow you. As their bodies enter the water, they are instantly transformed into dolphins! You look at your own body and are shocked to see that sleek gray flippers have replaced your arms.

Although you are horrified at first, you learn to enjoy life in the waves. Before long, you can't remember what it felt like to walk, and after a few years, you even forget that you were once a human being.

The End

"Your parents are right," Zeus explains. "They've discovered Olympus, and they've found my throne."

"But no one believes them! How can they prove they're right?" you ask.

Zeus grins mischievously. "If your parents really want clues, they will have to ask me themselves."

"But they won't!" you cry with frustration. "My grandmother already suggested they ask you for help. *I'm* not going to be able to convince them."

"But you won't have to," Zeus goes on, "because I'm going to pay them a visit myself. Here, take my hand."

When Zeus raises his other hand to the sky, thunder rumbles and one lightning bolt after another strikes the earth around you. You clutch Zeus with fear as the lightning flashes again and again.

"Athena's way of traveling was a little less nerve-racking," you shout.

Zeus lowers his hand, and the lightning disappears. You find yourself on your own doorstep. "Ring the doorbell," he tells you.

For the rest of your life, you will never forget the look on your parents' faces when they opened the door and saw Zeus.

The End

100

Quick! You have to think of a way to rescue Dionysus!

You drag a heavy urn of oil to the railing and shove it overboard. The urn hits the water with a loud splash. The sailors guarding Dionysus immediately abandon their watch to look over the side of the boat. You run to Dionysus and quietly begin to untie him.

You are still fumbling with the first knot when the sailors notice you. In less than a minute, you, too, are tied to the mast and gagged. Dionysus catches your eye and winks. You can't understand why he doesn't appear at all frightened. You struggle to free yourself, but one of the sailors hits you so hard that you black out.

Turn to page 111.

Trying to rescue Persephone seems too dangerous, so you decide to escape alone.

After dropping off a group of souls on Hades's side of the river, you guide the boat back to the other side. Without a moment's hesitation, you leap onto the shore and race away from the river. Charon stumbles ashore and calls your name, but he is too feeble to catch up with you. You run as fast as you can past dreary expanses of gray stone and out of the chasm.

You collapse on the sweet-smelling grass and gaze up at the sky, marveling at the intensity of the colors around you. Suddenly you notice a tall, bearded man striding toward you.

"I've been keeping track of your adventures," he says warmly, "and I must say, you've kept me entertained."

"Who are you?" you ask suspiciously.

"I thought you'd know. I'm Zeus."

Your mouth drops open. "Did you know I was looking for you?"

Zeus laughs. "Yes, and I know what's on your mind. Come on, I'll show you around Olympus."

Turn to the next page.

Right before your eyes, Zeus changes into a silvery stallion. You climb onto his back and he gallops off. Within minutes, the stallion stops at a huge table surrounded by twelve giant thrones. When you dismount, Zeus returns to his former appearance.

He offers you incredible food, like none you've ever tasted, and shows you exquisite shells scattered along his personal beach. He points out the landmarks of Olympus and reveals his secret treasures.

"There," he says, "I've shown you everything you need to make your parents' excavation successful beyond all dreams." He waves his hand before your eyes and whispers, "Now sleep."

You awaken in your own bed, feeling certain that if only your parents will listen to you, Zeus's directions will help them discover where the evidence is buried.

The End

Although you don't know exactly how you will rescue Persephone once you return to Hades's palace, you decide to leave Charon immediately. You tell him you want to take a break, and you push past the next group of souls trudging off the raft toward the palace.

But in your haste to return to Persephone, you stumble on the rocky ground. You twist your ankle and pause to rub it. Suddenly you notice a young man running a few hundred yards behind you. He moves so swiftly that his feet barely touch the ground! You wonder why anyone else would be so eager to reach the palace of Hades. Then you realize: he could be chasing you.

If you decide to find out who the runner is,
turn to page 110.

If you think it's safest to hide from him,
turn to page 128.

106

You don't want to get involved in Daedalus's flying plans, but to get around on your own, you'll need to look like an islander. You find clothing drying on the rocks and exchange it for your own. Even so, you soon discover that without Icarus and Daedalus, it is difficult to find your way around the island. You ask people you meet for directions to Olympus, but everyone says that mortal beings cannot approach the home of the gods without an invitation from Zeus. And no one knows how to find Zeus. After several days of searching, you become very discouraged.

Go on to the next page.

While walking along a rocky mountain path late one evening, you hear someone calling for help. You follow the cries to a gully, where a boy is trapped.

"I'll be right back as soon as I find something to help you with," you assure him before running off to get a fallen tree limb. You dangle it into the gorge and hold on tight as the boy climbs up the limb.

Turn to page 60.

108

Before you can ask about your parents' excavation, you find yourself whirling through time with Icarus. When you return to the twenty-first century, your parents are so astonished by the ancient coins Icarus carries that they believe your account of time travel. They adopt Icarus and abandon their archaeological research. Icarus becomes an instant celebrity. Even you become famous for your experiences in ancient Greece, and you and Icarus remain friends for the rest of your lives.

The End

110

You decide to risk finding out who the runner is. As you limp toward him, you notice small wings on each of his sandals. He waves to you as he approaches.

"Who are you? Where are you going?" you call warily.

He pauses, and you notice he's not at all out of breath. "I'm Hermes, son of Zeus and messenger of the gods. I'm on my way to get Persephone," he explains. "My father has ordered Hades to let her return to the Land of the Living."

"I was just on my way to rescue Persephone, too," you reply.

"Let me take care of getting Persephone." Hermes glances at your injured ankle, which has begun to swell. "I guess you're a living mortal after all. Your clothes are so strange that from a distance I couldn't tell *what* you were. As soon as I pick up Persephone, you can tell me where you come from and how you ended up in the Underworld. Wait right here and I'll bring you to the Land of the Living."

Turn to page 22.

When you regain consciousness, you wonder for a second if you have been taken to a jungle. There are grapevines everywhere you look. Lions, panthers, and bears prowl the deck, snarling occasionally at the terrified sailors—who waste no time in jumping overboard. In the midst of this craziness, Dionysus dances gleefully and plays a flute.

When the last sailor has disappeared into the sea, Dionysus claps his hands and the wild animals vanish. He unties you and thanks you for trying to help him.

"Are you the *god* Dionysus?" you ask in awe.

"Yes," he replies. "And I'd like to offer you a reward. As you may know, grapes are one of my specialties. If you'd like to take over raising grapes for the gods, Zeus would surely make you a demigod. Demigods are not immortal, but you would have a few special powers."

"On the summer solstice, could I visit my family in the twenty-first century?" you ask.

"Certainly," Dionysus replies.

You spend the rest of your life on Olympus, where you raise grapes of unearthly sweetness. You become well acquainted with Zeus and the other gods, although Dionysus remains your closest friend. Each year, on the summer solstice, you visit your family in Athens and give them information that advances their archaeological dig. When you are old, you look back on your experiences and conclude that you had as happy a life as anyone could want.

The End

112

He nods and smiles kindly. "I'm sorry about Icarus, but this is the way he has to die. Remember, he will be immortalized in poems and paintings, music and legends."

"I know," you answer sadly.

"I think you've had enough adventures. I'm going to take you back to your own century," says Zeus.

"But wait!" you cry. It is too late. You are already passing through the twilight shadows of time.

When you arrive at the Parthenon, you find yourself clutching a detailed map of Olympus revealing all your parents need to know for their dig to succeed. After examining the map intently, you walk through the streets of Athens to your home. You're just in time for breakfast.

The End

After leaving Hercules, you find a job in Mycenae so that you'll be able to finance your quest for Zeus. A goldsmith named Vasily hires you to sweep the shop and run errands. You don't make much money, so you pester Vasily into teaching you his craft. As he shows you how to fashion startlingly beautiful jewelry, your memories of your family fade and your interest in finding Zeus diminishes. By the time you're as fine a craftsman as Vasily himself, you have put aside all thoughts of Zeus.

Years later, a tall, regal man enters the shop and admires your work. He commissions a crown so luxurious that you say, "With a crown like this, you'll rival Zeus!"

The man laughs. "But I am Zeus!"

"Years ago, I was determined to find you so I could help my parents prove they'd discovered the ruins of Olympus," you reply, amazed.

"Yes, I know," replies Zeus. "Your grandmother keeps me informed when we get together on the summer solstice. Your parents are still working on the excavation. They've unearthed a few items— enough to continue the project—but not enough really to prove their discovery."

"Are they still worried about me?"

"Certainly. Your grandmother knows where you are," Zeus explains, "but your parents don't believe her. Would you like to return to the twenty-first century?"

Turn to page 116.

"I would never help you trap Hercules!" you tell Poseidon. You sound braver than you really feel.

Poseidon tightens his grip. "Very well, you will become my servant. I warn you, I will always have an eye on you."

As part of the underwater housekeeping team, you travel everywhere with Poseidon. You sweep broken shells, stray bits of seaweed, dead fish, and all kinds of debris out of the ocean and onto beaches.

One morning, as you wash driftwood onto the shores of Lemnos, you notice that Poseidon is not with you. A dolphin explains that there was a storm brewing over the Atlantic. Poseidon had to leave suddenly to warn the whales he had stationed there. He was too hurried to take his housekeeping team.

You wonder if you should take advantage of Poseidon's absence to escape. You don't know if you'll ever have another chance. But what will happen if you're caught? Besides, you keep hoping that one day you'll have the opportunity to sweep the shores of Olympus and find Zeus.

If you decide you're better off waiting,
turn to page 55.

If you decide to escape, turn to page 123.

116

You hesitate. You're perfectly content with your life in Mycenae. "No," you reply, "but would you give my family a message?"

Six months later, your parents unearth a golden crown that is not only magnificent but also remarkably well preserved. They are even more astonished when they notice a message inscribed along the edge. With breathless excitement, they read about your fate and examine your signature intently. When they show your grandmother the crown, she only smiles.

The End

After delivering the Bull of Minos and the red cattle to the king of Mycenae, you and Hercules begin your search for the Daughters of the Evening Land. They prove to be every bit as elusive as Zeus. You spend more than a year exploring countless islands as well as the mainland of Greece.

One night, when you are ready to collapse with exhaustion, you notice an enticing fragrance floating in the air. The two of you follow the scent to a silver lattice fence that surrounds a garden filled with mysterious night-blooming flowers and softly humming bees. Right away you know that it's the Evening Land.

Stepping over the fence, you feel deeply serene and refreshed. You can't recall ever having felt so wonderful. You pass many trees laden with unfamiliar fruit, but none of them have golden apples.

Three young women wearing wreaths around their heads walk toward you. "We are the Daughters of the Evening Land," one of them says graciously.

Without so much as a nod of greeting, Hercules says, "I'm looking for the golden apples."

Turn to the next page.

The Daughters look at each other in anguish. "Take any fruit, any flower, but please leave us the golden apples," they plead.

Hercules strides past the women to a tree bearing shining gold apples. Around the tree lies a hissing dragon with many heads. One of the dragon's heads opens its jaws and small tongues of flame dart toward you.

"Please, Hercules, let's forget about the apples," you suggest nervously. "I think the king of Mycenae will be satisfied with another kind of fruit."

"Hand me an arrow," says Hercules with cold determination.

"I don't like this at all," you insist. "Let's leave the apples alone."

"An arrow, now," says Hercules.

If you refuse and walk toward the Daughters of the Evening Land, turn to page 56.

If you reluctantly give Hercules an arrow, turn to page 125.

120

"If you value your life, you will not drive the Chariot of the Sun," Helios warns. "Please! Choose anything else!"

But you and Phaeton insist, and at last Helios woefully relents. It's dawn, so you have to hurry. You climb into the gleaming gold chariot that carries the sun and grab the reins. Even before you can say goodbye to Helios, the horses are racing through the clouds.

You gaze down upon the earth and the wind rushes against your face. As the chariot climbs higher, you find it hard to breathe. You are higher than you've ever flown in a plane!

Suddenly the chariot lurches to the right, then swings wildly to the left. The horses gallop faster than ever.

"Tighten the reins!" Phaeton shouts.

Turn to page 122.

"I am! I am!" you shriek, but you can't control the horses. They rush up and down like a nightmarish roller coaster. The chariot plunges so close to the earth that some mountains catch fire! Soon thick smoke is billowing all around you. Flames lick the wheels of the chariot, and you realize that you've set a path of fire blazing across the earth!

A bolt of lightning flashes through the smoke.

Phaeton screams as the golden chariot shatters. You plunge to your death, never knowing that you finally succeeded in attracting the attention of Zeus, who threw the lightning bolt to prevent you from destroying the rest of the earth.

The End

You tell no one about your plan to escape; you just move on to other shores to go about your work as usual. Toward the end of the day, you sweep the hull of a shipwrecked boat onto a beach. Instead of sliding quickly back with the waves, as you are supposed to, you scurry inside the hull and hide.

From the beach, you can see an enormous table about twenty feet long and very high. There are gigantic thrones along one side of the table. You can't believe your eyes! One of the thrones looks exactly like the one your parents discovered. Could you really have been so lucky as to have found Olympus?

Just as you climb out from under the hull to investigate, a powerful, icy wave grabs your ankles and knocks you to the ground. As you slide past the foam into the depths of the ocean, you recognize the force as the hand of Poseidon himself.

Water rushes into your lungs. You're not at all surprised to realize that you can no longer breathe underwater.

The End

You agree to help Poseidon trap Hercules. The sea god carries you back to the place where you were swimming. "Pretend you're drowning. Scream for help," he instructs you.

"Hercules!" you shout as loudly as you can. "Help me, Hercules!"

In less than a minute, you see Hercules run toward the beach. "I'm drowning!" you cry. Poseidon yanks you underwater a few times as Hercules swims toward you.

Suddenly, you feel Poseidon release you. A second later, Hercules is thrashing around in a desperate struggle with the liquid green god.

"Let go of me, Poseidon," warns Hercules, "or I'll show you who really rules the ocean."

To free himself from Poseidon's grip, Hercules begins moving one arm in fast, powerful circles, churning up the water. You watch in horror as a whirlpool forms in front of Hercules. It grows larger and larger until it sweeps you underwater.

This time, you can't speak or breathe. For a few seconds you are conscious of bubbles rushing around you before you're lost to the world.

The End

You pull an arrow out of the quiver and hand it to Hercules. He takes it and shoots it into the dragon's heart. The creature shrieks and writhes before it collapses. As Hercules gathers the golden apples, the Daughters of the Evening Land weep sorrowfully. After he picks the last apple, the enchanted garden sinks into the earth, leaving only the three women and a trace of the mysterious fragrance.

"Come on," says Hercules. "Let's take these apples back to Mycenae." You turn and follow, but each step makes you sadder.

Suddenly you seize the bag of apples from Hercules and begin running back to where the Evening Land disappeared.

"What are you doing?" Hercules calls as he chases you. "Are you crazy?"

Turn to the next page.

126

Perhaps you *are* crazy, but you feel you have to return the stolen apples. Hercules catches up with you and wrestles you to the ground. You cling to the bag stubbornly, but Hercules hits you hard. Just as you drop the apples, a bearded man yanks Hercules away from you.

"Zeus!" exclaims Hercules.

"That's enough!" snaps Zeus. "I expected you to show more patience with a visitor from another century."

Zeus helps you to your feet and explains, "Hercules must do his tasks. Stealing is detestable, but it is his destiny. It is noble of you to try to interfere, but I cannot allow you to succeed."

Go on to the next page.

You nod your head. "Are my parents destined to prove they've discovered Olympus?"

Zeus smiles kindly and puts his arm around you. "With your help, your parents will become more famous than they dare to dream." He touches your forehead—and instantly, you are home.

The excavation takes longer than expected, but at last you discover the treasures of Olympus, including the golden apples Hercules stole. The museum in Athens exhibits most of these riches, but you keep one of the apples as a souvenir of your ancient adventures.

The End

128

You duck behind a boulder. As the young man speeds past, you think you see small wings on his sandals.

Your ankle becomes so swollen that you must spend a couple of days resting in a cave. Finally you reach the gates of Hades's palace and slip inside. To your surprise, the thrones of Persephone and Hades are both empty. Before you have a chance to wonder where they are, cold and powerful hands grab you from behind.

Twisting your head, you see that it's Hades himself. "Where's Persephone?" you ask.

"She's gone!" he replies angrily. "Zeus sent his messenger, Hermes, to bring Persephone back to the Land of the Living. They left just a few days ago."

You can't believe your ears. The runner you saw must have been Hermes!

"But in spite of Zeus's efforts, Persephone will be back," says Hades with an evil grin. "Even though she was never hungry, I made her eat a few pomegranate seeds. Now that she's eaten the fruit of the Underworld, she has to spend part of each year with me."

Go on to the next page.

As he talks, Hades drags you down a dark stairway. He unlocks a door at the bottom and thrusts you inside. "I'm glad you'll be here to keep Persephone company, although I'll have to keep you locked up from now on. Don't worry, my servants will take good care of you. But I can never let you leave this dungeon, now that I know how clever you are."

The End

ABOUT THE ARTIST

Marco Cannella was born in Ascoli Piceno, Italy, on September 29, 1972. Marco started his career in art as a decorator and an illustrator when he was a college student. He became a full-time professional in 2001 when he received the flag-prize for the "Palio della Quintana" (one of the most important Italian historical games). Since then, he has worked as an illustrator at Studio Inventario in Bologna. He has also been a scenery designer for professional theater companies. He works for the production company ASP srl in Rome as a character designer and set designer on the preproduction of a CG feature film. In 2004 he moved to Bangalore, India, to serve as full-time art director on this project.

ABOUT THE AUTHOR

When she was growing up, **Deborah Lerme Goodman** wanted to be a painter in a Parisian garret. That never happened, but other interesting things did. In addition to writing *The Magic of the Unicorn,* she has written four other books in the original *Choose Your Own Adventure* series, two children's books for the Smithsonian Institution, and many magazine articles, mostly about textiles. She has directed community schools, led a mayor's office, studied Chinese and lived in China, and finally got her dream job—teaching English to adult immigrants. She lives in Cambridge, Massachusetts, with her husband, John.

For games, activities, and other fun stuff, or to write to Chooseco, visit us online at CYOA.com.

Throne of Zeus Trivia Quiz

You got the proof you needed from Zeus, but what other mythical nuggets remain uncovered? Climb up Mount Olympus and see what else you can dig up, by correctly answering the questions below!

1) **What is your parents' occupation?**
   A. Architects
   B. Archivists
   C. Archaeologists
   D. Archenemies

2) **When has your grandmother spoken to Zeus?**
   A. Summer solstice
   B. Vernal equinox
   C. Your birthday
   D. International Talk Like A Pirate Day

3) **Who helps you travel back in time to ancient Greece?**
   A. Zeus
   B. Athena
   C. Artemis
   D. The security guard at the Parthenon

4) **What is the name of the beast that inhabits the Labyrinth?**
   A. Zorba
   B. David Bowie
   C. King Minos
   D. Minotaur

5) **What do Daedalus and Icarus use to construct their wings?**
   A. Construction paper and duct tape
   B. Feathers, thread, and clay
   C. Feathers, thread, and donkey dung
   D. Feathers, thread, and wax

6) **Helios is god of...**
   A. The Underworld
   B. The sun
   C. The harvest
   D. The phaeton

7) **What are you doing when you first meet Hercules?**
   A. Guarding the Bull of Minos
   B. Sweeping shells for Poseidon
   C. Ferrying dead souls with Charon
   D. Eating a pomegranate with Persephone

8) **What animal form does Zeus take in *The Throne of Zeus*?**
   A. Dolphin
   B. Stallion
   C. Bull
   D. A and B

9) **What do the sailors plan to do with Dionysus?**
   A. Worship him
   B. Return him to Naxos
   C. Kidnap him
   D. Make him walk the plank

10) **What special tool does Hermes use to deliver messages between the gods?**
   A. Winged sandals
   B. Reliable high-speed internet connection
   C. A magical flute that plays the gods' messages back to the recipient
   D. The post office

THE TRUMPET OF TERROR

CHOOSE FROM 28 ENDINGS!

BY DEBORAH LERME GOODMAN